DO YOU KNOW WHERE I AM?

By Anne Abernathy Hahn

Illustrated by Lynn Armstrong Hirsch

DERRYDALE BOOKS
New York • Avenel, New Jersey

Dedicated to:
CHRISTOPHER, MIKAEL, LAUREN, WILLIAM and DAVID

Published by Derrydale Books,
distributed by Outlet Book Company, Inc.,
a Random House Company,
40 Engelhard Avenue,
Avenel, New Jersey 07001.

Printed and Bound in the United States of America.

Library of Congress Cataloging-in-Publication Data

Hahn, Anne Abernathy.
Do you know where I am? / by Anne Abernathy Hahn ; illustrated by
Lynn Armstrong Hirsch.
p.   cm.
Summary: Text gives a clue to a child's location, and by turning
the page the reader sees the answer in a picture.
ISBN 0-517-07394-3 :
[1. Hide-and-seek—Fiction. 2. Literary recreations.]
I. Hirsch, Lynn Armstrong, ill. II. Title.
PZ7.H1249Do   1992
[E]—dc20   92-11189
                                                        CIP
                                                        AC

8 7 6 5 4 3 2 1

I wiggle my toes in the soft, cool sand
and watch the seagulls fly

out beyond land.

The sand and the water tickle my toes...
Should I wear a big hat, or get sun on my nose?
Shall I go for a swim, or build castles so high?
The breeze in the sea oats

sounds just like a sigh....

DO YOU KNOW WHERE I AM?

HERE I AM!
At The Beach!

Oh, the sounds I can hear—

         Tee-hee-whee and *ca-caw!*

And the roar of a lion, just stretching his jaw.

There's a monkey who's got a banana to eat,

And—ooh!—a big snake—

         Do they ever eat meat?

Giant plants, vines, and parrots,

         and steamy, hot air,

A place for adventure . . .

         Can you find my bear?

DO YOU KNOW

WHERE I AM?

HERE I AM!
In The Jungle!

I can't talk too loud,

                so I'll whisper to you . . .

This is one of my favorite things to do.

I come here to read and to find a good book,

There are shelves full of good ones —

                Just look! and Oh! Look!

My mom helps me check out whatever I seek

Now, on home to read —

                and we'll come back next week!

DO YOU KNOW WHERE I AM?

HERE I AM!
In The Library!

Splish and then **splash**

and then **booble-di-boo,**

This feels so refreshing—

there's so much to do!

There are millions of bubbles

piled up all around,

I can stack them up high on my head, I have found.

My duck swims in circles,

Mom shampoos my hair,

If I splash **really** hard

I might scare my pet bear!

DO YOU KNOW

WHERE I AM?

HERE I AM!
In The Bathtub!

I can't see the cooks,

but I *can* smell their cooking!

Oh, what shall I choose?

It is all yummy looking!

Shall I have some fried chicken, potatoes and beans,

or a great big ham sandwich

with fruit and with greens,

or a plate of spaghetti, and maybe some cake?

And then wash it all down

with a chocolate milk shake. . . .

DO YOU KNOW WHERE I AM?

HERE I AM!
In A Restaurant!

We line up for tickets,

    Then walk right on in,

Beside other boys and girls, and women and men.

The popcorn is popping,

    there's candy—and more!

Then it's dark as nighttime

    when you go through the door.

I find a good seat and then sit up real tall,

And a picture comes on

    that's as BIG as a wall!

DO YOU KNOW WHERE I AM?

HERE I AM!
At The Movie Theater!

"ALL ABOARD! Tickets, please!,"
                    the conductor soon calls,
We climb up the steps
                    and take seats, one and all.
We hear a loud whistle, and start soon enough
To move down the steel tracks
                    with a *chugg* and a *chuff.*
We go faster and faster
                    and faster than fast
And we sit and look out
                    as the country speeds past....

DO YOU KNOW

WHERE I AM?

HERE I AM!
On A Train!

I stand up on the scale
        to see what I weigh,
And get measured to find
        what my height is today.
The people in white coats
        examine my nose,
And my throat, eyes and ears,
        and my knees and my toes.
With a cold metal circle, they check out my chest . . .
And give me a lollipop—
        That's what I like best!

DO YOU KNOW WHERE I AM?

HERE I AM!
At The Doctor's Office!

What great adventures!

What fan-ta-bu-lous fun!

I gather my friends,

and say "G'night!" to the sun.

I set down my boat, my train, and my truck,

And give thanks for my safety,

and thanks for my luck,

And thanks for my family, all of us fed,

And our house, and my room,

and my snuggly bed....

DO YOU KNOW

WHERE I AM?

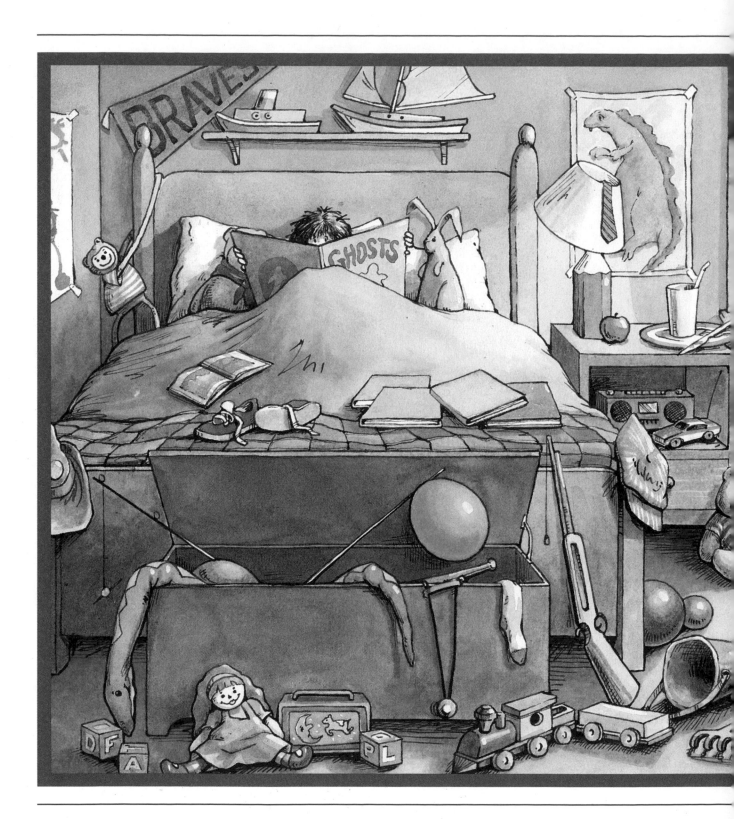